MY COUNTRY, 'TIS OF THEE

SCHOLASTIC INC.

New York   Toronto   London   Auckland   Sydney   Mexico City   New Delhi   Hong Kong   Buenos Aires

Photography credits for *My Country 'Tis of Thee*:
Cover: FPG by Getty Images; Back cover: Jim Cummins/FPG by Getty Images
Pages 2-3: Superstock; 4: Superstock; 5: Jim Cummins/FPG by Getty Images; 6: Peter Gridley/FPG by Getty Images;
7: top row, second from left and far right: FPG by Getty Images; all others: Superstock; 8: Superstock; 9: Superstock;
10–11: Stan Osolinski/Superstock; 12: Getty Images; 13: Bob Glander/FPG by Getty Images; 14, all: Superstock; 15: Superstock;
16: Superstock; 17, background: Superstock; 17, left: Jeff Greenberg/PhotoEdit; 17, right: Tony Freeman/PhotoEdit; 18: Superstock;
19: Superstock; 20: Superstock; 21: Superstock; 22–23: Superstock; 24: Mark Peterson/Corbis Saba.

ISBN 0-439-39195-4

10 9 8 7 6 5 4 3   02 03 04 05 06

Printed in the U.S.A.   08
First printing, September 2002

My country, 'tis of thee,

"Still whatever fate betide us

Children of the flag are we!"

Sweet land of liberty,
Of thee I sing;

Land where my fathers died!

Land of the Pilgrim's pride!

From ev'ry mountainside,

Let freedom ring!

My native country, thee,

Bill of Rights

Congress of the United States,

begun and held at the City of, New York, on

Wednesday, the fourth of March, one thousand seven hundred and eighty nine.

The Conventions of a number of the States having, at the time of their adopting the Constitution, expressed a desire, in order to prevent misconstruction or abuse of its powers, that further declaratory and restrictive clauses should be added: And as extending the ground of public confidence in the Government, will best insure the beneficent ends of its institution:

Resolved, by the SENATE and HOUSE of REPRESENTATIVES of the UNITED STATES of AMERICA in Congress assembled, two thirds of both Houses concurring, That the following Articles be proposed to the Legislatures of the several States, as Amendments to the Constitution of the United States; all, or any of which articles, when ratified by three fourths of the said Legislatures, to be valid to all intents and purposes, as part of the said Constitution; viz.

ARTICLES in addition to, and Amendment of the Constitution of the United States of America, proposed by Congress, and ratified by the Legislatures of the several States, pursuant to the fifth Article of the Original Constitution.

Article the first ...... After the first enumeration required by the first Article of the Constitution, there shall be one Representative for every thirty thousand, until the number shall amount to one hundred, after which, the proportion shall be so regulated by Congress, that there shall be not less than one hundred Representatives, nor less than one Representative for every forty thousand persons, until the number of Representatives shall amount to two hundred, after which, the proportion shall be so regulated by Congress, that there shall not be less than two hundred Representatives, nor more than one Representative for every fifty thousand persons.

Land of the noble free,
Thy name I love;

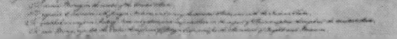

I love thy rocks and rills,

Thy woods and templed hills.

My heart with rapture thrills
Like that above.

My country, 'tis of thee,
Sweet land of liberty,
Of thee I sing;
Land where my fathers died!
Land of the Pilgrim's pride!
From ev'ry mountainside,
Let freedom ring!
My native country, thee,
Land of the noble free,
Thy name I love;
I love thy rocks and rills,
Thy woods and templed hills.
My heart with rapture thrills
Like that above.